Tatty
Ratty

For Pandora

First published in Great Britain by Doubleday,
an imprint of Transworld Publishers,
a division of the Random House Group Ltd, 2001
Color separations by Bright Arts, Hong Kong
Printed and bound in Belgium by Proost NV
Designed by Ian Butterworth
First American edition, 2002
1 3 5 7 9 10 8 6 4 2

Library of Congress Cataloging-in-Publication Data
Cooper, Helen (Helen F.)
  Tatty Ratty / Helen Cooper.— 1st American ed.
    p. cm.
  Summary: When Molly's stuffed rabbit gets lost, she and her parents
imagine all the adventures it is having before returning home.
  ISBN 0-374-37386-8
  [1. Lost and found possessions—Fiction. 2. Rabbits—Fiction.
3. Toys—Fiction. 4. Imagination—Fiction.] I. Title.

PZ7.C78555 Tat 2002
[E]—dc21

                                                        2001017055

Tatty Ratty

Helen Cooper

BUS?

BED?

sofa?

Farrar Straus Giroux

New York

Tatty Ratty was lost again.
"When did you see him last?"
said Mom.
"In the kitchen," sniffed Molly.
"And then on the bus."
"And after the bus?" groaned Mom.
"I don't know," sobbed Molly.

"Let's look for him," said Mom.
So they went and looked in the usual places,
the sorts of places they'd found him before:
under the sofa, behind the bed —
but they couldn't see a whisker or paw of him.

Mom called the bus company.
"No, we haven't found anything yet,"
said the man on the phone.
"What are we going to do?" wailed Molly.
"I can't sleep without Tatty Ratty."

"You can sleep with us so you won't
be lonely," said Mom.
"Tatty Ratty'll be lonely on the bus,"
worried Molly.

"Maybe he'll hop off,"
whispered Dad.

"He might," said Molly, snuggling down.
"He'll find a train and drive it home."

"Will he wear a uniform?" murmured Dad.
"Not a whole uniform," Molly yawned.
"When I first got him, he had blue buttons.
That's all he'd need."

"Tatty Ratty's driving a train,"
Dad told Mom the next morning.

"Not anymore," said Molly.
"He's having porridge
with the Three Bears.
He's eating . . . and eating . . .
and getting fat."

But that night, at bath time, Molly said,
"I want Tatty Ratty."
"Isn't he with the Three Bears?" said Mom.

"Not anymore," said Molly.
"He ate so much his stuffing hurt.
Now he's coming home, with Cinderella."

"Mmmm," said Mom. "She'll clean him up.
She'll mend all his holes and brush his fur."

"He won't like it,"
warned Molly.

Molly knew what Tatty Ratty
would do. He'd bite Cinderella
if she brushed his fur.
He'd scrabble, and scuttle,
right through the window,
and bounce down a mountain,
into the sea.

She told Mom what would happen.

"What a bad rabbit," said Mom.
"Well, at least he'll be clean. But I hope he can swim."

Molly said,
"Pirates will save him.
He'll sail on their boat,
and peep at their treasure,
and sneak a look at their secret map,
and then . . .
he'll know the way home."

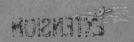

EXTENSION

It was time for bed,
but Molly said,
"I won't sleep without
Tatty Ratty."
"He's busy reading that map,"
said Mom.
"Not anymore," said Molly.

"The pirates didn't like
sharing their map, so they

strung

him

up

by

his

bunny

ears!"

"He'll find a way to escape,"
said Mom. "He always does."

"A dragon will save him," said Dad.

"It'll swoop down, just like this . . .

. . . and lift Tatty Ratty like this . . ."

Molly yelled, "He'll be cold in the sky!"

"He'll grow more fur," said Dad.

Molly growled, "Will he come home on the dragon?"

"Not when you're making that noise," said Dad.

"Dragons like peace and quiet."

"So where will they go?" said Molly.

"They'll fly to the moon,"

said Dad.

"And will the Man in the Moon
be there?"

"Oh, indeed he will," said Dad.
"He'll roll Tatty Ratty
in moondust
till his fur turns sugary white."

"He'll like that," murmured Molly.

Molly dreamed of a spaceship.
It belonged to the
Man in the Moon
and it zoomed across the sky,
with Tatty Ratty riding inside.

The spaceship hovered over Molly's town,
and Tatty Ratty bailed out.
Soon he drifted down . . .

. . . and down . . .

But before he landed,
Molly woke.

Molly told Mom her dream.
"That means he's almost home," sighed Mom.
"If you close your eyes and go to sleep,
we'll find him when the sun comes up."

The sun came up very early.

"I'm sure he's here somewhere," yawned Mom.

"Remember, he might look different," yawned Dad.

"Yes, he'll be wearing his buttons," said Molly.

"And all that porridge will have made him fat."

"He'll be very clean and fluffy," said Mom.

"I know," said Molly, "but he'll still be Tatty Ratty."

There were a lot of rabbits.

"What about this one?" said Dad.
"That's not Tatty Ratty," said Molly.

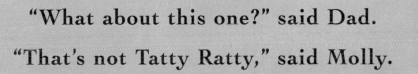

"Maybe this one?" said Mom.
"Don't be silly," said Molly.

"Look!" shouted Molly.

"He's pricked up his ears, and he's lovely and white."

"He's smiling at me!"

"About time, too,"
whispered Tatty Ratty.